For those with time to spare—
children, dogs, and jigsaw puzzlers

JIGSAW

MYSTERY IN THE MAIL

CANDLEWICK PRESS

First US edition 2022

Library of Congress Catalog Card Number 2021947893
ISBN 978-1-5362-2499-3

APS 27 26 25 24 23 22
10 9 8 7 6 5 4 3 2 1

Printed in Humen, Dongguan, China

This book was typeset in ITC Underwood.
The illustrations were done in watercolor and ink.

Candlewick Press
99 Dover Street
Somerville, Massachusetts 02144

www.candlewick.com

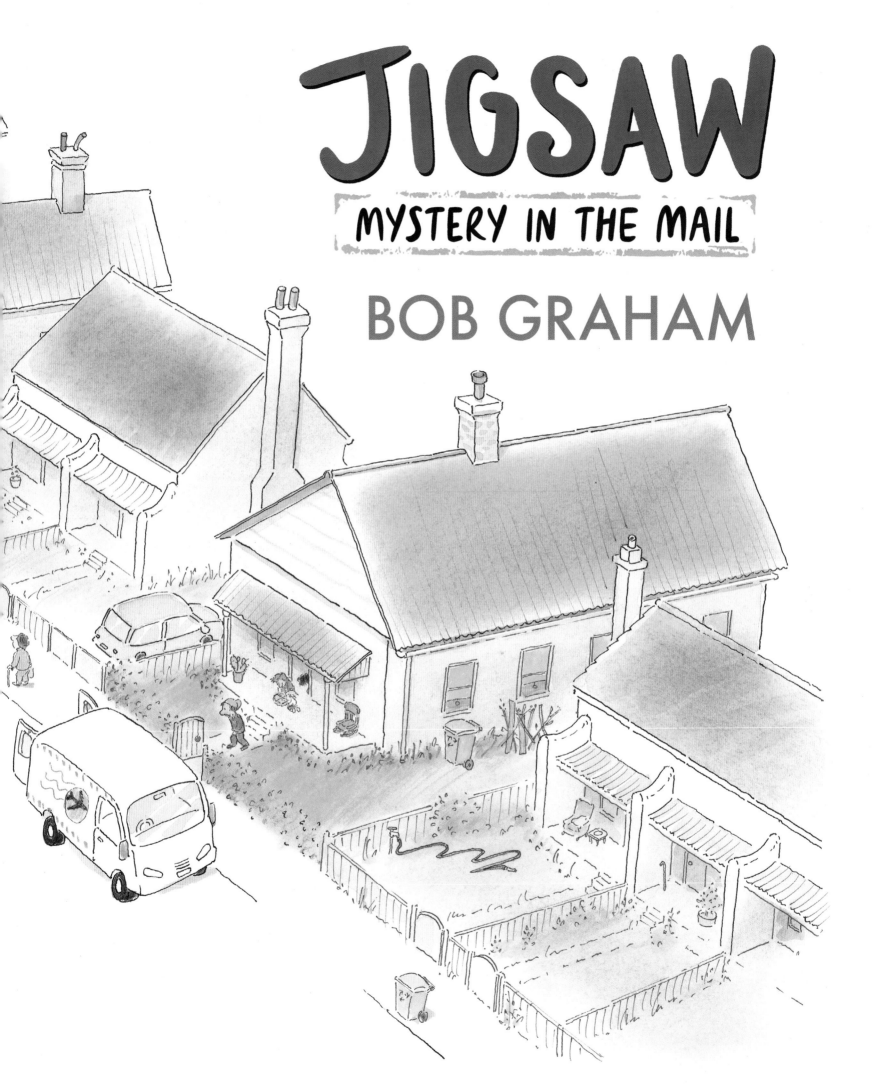

No one knew who sent it.

It arrived one day all covered with stamps.

A beautiful jigsaw—an African sunrise.

"Good luck to you all" was all the card said.

The Kellys stood there and undid the wrapping.

"Oh! Let's do it!" said Kitty and Katie and Mom.

"I've got time on my hands . . ." said Dad,

and set his watch to late autumn.

"Let's get started," said the Kellys.

Early in winter they completed the edges.

Kitty and Katie

and Lucy helped too.

The girls went out playing in spring and in summer,
but Dad kept his head down just getting it done.
With autumn approaching, they sorted the colors
as a beautiful dawn began to emerge.
"The hippo's swim shorts . . ." said Dad.

They looked high and low. They looked under Kitty.

They looked under Lucy and everywhere else.

Then Mom stopped, and she thought.

Yes, she did some hard thinking . . .

"I think I've got it!" said Mom.

"Where is it?" they said.

"Went out in the trash?" she whispered.

"We'll find it," Dad said,

"if it takes us all autumn."

"Oh! Let's do it," said Kitty

and Katie and Mom.

Dad looked at his watch,

and the leaves started falling.

"Jigsaw piece missing; Hippo's swim shorts," Dad said,
and the man stroked his chin. "Yes! People come looking,
but they don't often find them. Try the pile at the end."

"Some hope's what we need, to see things a bit clearer."

"Let's start here, then," said Katie. "Shouldn't take long."

There were letters of love from faraway places, letters of sorrow, notes of forgiveness, bus tickets, train tickets, cards saying "thank you," and newspapers old and forgotten in time.

Old confetti from weddings, a sock no one wanted,

a note that said, "I'll meet you at twenty to nine"

and "Sorry for your troubles" (attached to old flowers).

"Get well," said another, sealed with a kiss.

There were shopping lists—too many to mention—
an old soldier's photo yellow with age,
and every so often a breeze would lift them
and put them back down like falling rain.

The Kellys looked up; they looked down,

"Let's look at it this way," said Dad.

"It's waiting around and will find us again."

"That's wishful thinking," said Mom.

"Let's wish, then," said Katie . . .

and they sadly
went home.

Through the front door, back into the kitchen.

It was Dad's boot
that had now lost it . . .

It was Kitty who found it.

"Can't believe that we missed it.

Must have been there the whole time."

So with autumn here with them,
the puzzle was finished.

It was Kitty who placed it,
her sister who straightened it.

The hippo found his swim shorts,
and the sun came up out of Africa.

To whoever it was who sent them the puzzle,

Katie wrote back (with pictures by Kitty).

Our love
to you too
and hope this
card finds you
Katie and Kitty
Kelly

To: Our jigsaw Sender
Adress: ~~Nowear~~ Sumwear

She addressed it to "Nowear," and Mom said,

"Well, they have to live somewhere."

So Katie changed it to "Sumwear."

With enough stamps to cover its travels . . .

and with a hope and a wish and a "shouldn't take long,"
they went out into the autumn twilight.

Kitty dropped it in the mailbox.

A small boat on a wide ocean of letters.